Bears Beware

PATRICIA REILLY GIFF

Bears Beware

illustrated by

ALASDAIR BRIGHT

WENDY
LAMB
BOOKS

Visit us on the Web! randomhouse.com/kids
Educators and librarians, for a variety of teaching tools, visit us at randomhouse.com/teachers

Library of Congress Cataloging-in-Publication Data
Giff, Patricia Reilly.
Bears beware / Patricia Reilly Giff ; illustrated by Alasdair Bright. — 1st ed.
p. cm. — (Zigzag Kids ; #5)
Summary: Mitchell is afraid when the children from the Zigzag Center go camping overnight, but he tries to be brave and discovers that nature is not so scary after all.
ISBN 978-0-385-73889-7 (trade) — ISBN 978-0-385-90756-9 (lib. bdg.) —
ISBN 978-0-375-85913-7 (pbk.) — ISBN 978-0-375-89639-2 (ebook)
[1. Camping—Fiction. 2. Fear—Fiction. 3. Schools—Fiction.]
I. Bright, Alasdair, ill. II. Title.
PZ7.G3626Bd 2012
[Fic]—dc22
2011003997

Printed in the United States of America
10 9 8 7 6 5 4 3 2 1
First Edition

For my boys,
Jim and Bill,
with love
—P.R.G.

. . .

For my friend Jenny Goodes,
with love
—A.B.

Yolanda

Sumiko

Charlie

Destiny

Gina

Mitchell

Habib

Clifton

Trevor

Beebe

Angel

Peter

CHAPTER 1

MONDAY

School was over for the day. Whew!

It was time for the Zigzag Afternoon Center.

Mitchell McCabe darted into the lunchroom. He scooped up a snack from the counter.

It was some kind of bread thing. It had green stuff inside. The green stuff crunched against his teeth.

Mitchell gave his best friend, Habib, a poke. "Weird," he whispered.

The lunch lady must have heard. "I like to give out surprises all the time," she said.

"Dee-lightful," Gina said.

Mitchell and Habib grinned at each other. *Dee-lightful* was the music teacher's favorite word. Gina was in love with music.

Too bad she sang like a coyote.

The lunch lady was watching. Mitchell didn't want to hurt her feelings. He jammed the snack into his mouth.

Habib was juggling his snack. It left little green chunks on the floor. Mitchell watched him swoop down and juggle them up again.

"Come down to the auditorium, everyone," Ellie, one of the college helpers, called. "There's news! Great news!"

Mitchell crossed his fingers. "Maybe they're going to shut down the school," he said.

Habib stopped juggling. "Really?"

"I saw it on television. A huge snowstorm. Whoosh. No school."

"It's not winter," Habib said. "Not even close."

Mitchell nodded. Still, this was the best time for school to shut down. His birthday was at the end of the week. He would have the whole week to celebrate.

They passed the outside door. Mitchell looked around. Mrs. Farelli, the art teacher, would have a fit if he went out.

He took a chance. He needed fresh air to get rid of the snack taste.

He opened the door. A gust of air blew in. So did Popsicle sticks, an old homework paper, and—

Rain!

Enough for a bath.

Mitchell opened his mouth wide to catch a drop. *Ahhhhhh!*

"Shut the door!" Gina screamed behind them. "I'll catch the worst cold of my life. My grandma Maroni says I have a weak throat."

Habib grabbed his neck. "Your throat needs muscles. Take it to the gym."

"Not funny," Gina said.

"Listen," Mitchell told her. "We're going to hear big news in the auditorium. Who knows? The school might shut down. You could stay in bed all day."

"Maybe it's a trip to Hawaii," Habib said. "You could go away."

Mitchell slid across the floor. "Look out, waves. Here I come!"

Snap!

That was Mrs. Farelli. She was on her way down the hall.

She was a great finger snapper.

"Someone is using his outside voice inside the Afternoon Center," she said.

It was a good thing Mrs. Farelli was standing straight as a stick.

If she looked down, she'd see that homework paper floating in a rain puddle on the floor.

Mrs. Farelli turned. She went the other way.

"Dee-lightful," Habib said.

They dashed into the auditorium. Mitchell couldn't wait to hear the news.

His big sister, Angel, was in the front row. She was sitting with her friend Yolanda.

Ellie was standing on the stage.

Mr. Oakley, the grandfather who helped out, stood next to her. He was wearing his best jacket, with zigzag lines.

And there was Mitchell's teacher, Ms. Katz, with new purple eyeglasses.

Mrs. Farelli slid into a seat at the end of Mitchell's row. Her face was serious. And she was looking his way.

Mitchell tried to look serious, too. He frowned hard. His eyebrows half covered his eyes.

Ellie stepped forward. "Here's our news," she said.

Mitchell forgot to look serious. He crossed his fingers and his toes.

"No school, please," he said under his breath.

"Dee-lightful," Habib said.

CHAPTER 2

STILL MONDAY

Mitchell held his breath. What would he do with his free time?

It made him almost dizzy to think of it.

He'd write a story. He was pretty good at that.

Maybe it would be about a magician with all kinds of powers.

What would he call him?

Mitchell squinted up at the ceiling. Harry something.

No, someone had written about a Harry.

How about Gary? Gary Bopper. Great name.

Gary would have a beard and muscles. He'd be brave. And strong.

All the things Mitchell wasn't.

Mitchell snapped his fingers. Perfect.

Mrs. Farelli frowned. She leaned forward.

He'd forgotten. Mrs. Farelli liked to be the only finger snapper in the Center.

Mitchell looked up at the stage. He put on his listening face.

He thought about an adventure for Gary Bopper. Fighting a giant grizzly bear. The bear had claws that were sharp as knives.

Mitchell shivered.

Everyone began to clap.

Mitchell sat up straight.

"... old enough to leave home now," Ellie was saying.

What?

Mitchell didn't want to leave home. His mother would miss him. Who'd help his father carry out the trash? Who'd sleep with his dog, Maggie?

Worse yet, what about his birthday? What about his presents? What about his birthday cake?

Ellie smiled. "We'll stay overnight at the Zigzag Nature Center."

"Eee-ha!" Trevor, a kindergarten kid, yelled.

Mitchell leaned over to Habib. He didn't care if Mrs. Farelli saw him. "What about our mothers?"

Habib didn't answer. He was still listening.

Maybe Habib didn't care about leaving his mother.

Mitchell couldn't believe it. Habib's mother made the best chicken. Her cupcakes had gooey icing.

Mitchell didn't want Habib to think he was a baby, though. Mitchell's sister, Angel, called him that all the time.

"It's great news." Mitchell could hardly get the words out.

Who'd want to stay at the Nature Center? It was probably full of poison ivy.

Things might wander around in the woods. Bears, maybe. Coyotes. Snakes and lizards.

"Any questions?" Ellie asked.

Hands waved all over the place.

"Where will we sleep?" Charlie asked.

"In tents," Ellie said.

"Eee-ha!" Trevor yelled again.

A bear could rip open a tent in two minutes, Mitchell thought.

And wouldn't it be dark?

At home he slept with the hall light on.

He wanted to be sure things weren't moving around.

Creatures like the ones on the Nature Channel.

"We'll see nature up close," Ellie said.

"Dee-lightful," Gina said.

"You're right." Mr. Oakley stepped forward. He waved his hands around.

Mitchell hoped he wouldn't fall off the stage.

"We'll learn about unusual plants and animals." Mr. Oakley smiled. "We'll be surprised at all we see."

Mitchell tried a cough. It was an *I have to stay home* cough.

Mr. Oakley was still talking. "We might even see nature at night."

Mitchell's next cough was louder. It sounded like a clap of thunder.

Mrs. Farelli was passing permission slips around. She frowned at him.

Mitchell stopped coughing. He put on a Gary Bopper face. A *Don't worry about me, I'm only choking* face.

Mrs. Farelli looked as if she didn't believe him anyway.

Mitchell sat back.

He thought about tents in the dark. And paw prints.

Bears with teeth as large as their claws.

He thought about killer plants that grabbed your ankle.

Worst of all, spiders with fangs and feelers!

CHAPTER 3

SATURDAY MORNING

Mitchell and Angel were wearing long-sleeved shirts and pants. "We'll have to watch out for deer ticks," Mr. Oakley had said.

They dragged their bags down the street. Their dog, Maggie, raced around them. She thought it was a great adventure.

Mitchell didn't think it was so great. He'd hardly slept all night.

Mom walked with them. "Watch out for each other," she said about a hundred times.

"Don't worry," Angel said. "We'll be home by tomorrow afternoon."

By that time, Mitchell's birthday would be almost over.

"Keep an eye on each other anyway," Mom said.

Mitchell looked at Angel. She was older than he was. Taller. But her arms and legs were skinny as sticks.

What good would she be against a bear?

He shivered.

"Do you feel sick?" Mom asked.

Mitchell started to nod.

Angel was staring. "Are you going to be a baby?"

Mitchell put on a Gary Bopper face. "I'm almost as old as you are."

Up ahead was the Zelda A. Zigzag School. Mom gave them both a bunch of kisses.

Mitchell kept his head down. He didn't want the whole Afternoon Center to see.

He clumped his bag across the school yard. He clumped carefully. His bag was old. The zipper was a little broken.

His mother had put red tape all over the outside. "It'll be easy to spot," she'd said.

Afternoon Center kids were coming from everywhere.

Trevor was walking on stilts. "I'm going to keep away from snakes and poison ivy!" he yelled.

Destiny twirled across the yard. She had green beads in her hair. About fifty of them.

Mitchell wondered how she could hold her head up. It must be heavy.

Angel's friend Yolanda was right behind them. "Hey, guys!" she called. "Wait up."

Angel slowed down.

Mitchell sped away from them. He caught up to Habib.

Mr. Oakley stood next to the bus. He wore jeans and combat boots. He still looked like a grandfather.

"Hurry, everyone," Mr. Oakley said. "We don't want to miss a moment of fun."

"I can't hurry too much," Habib said. "I have a giant bag."

Mitchell looked down. Habib's bag was elephant-sized. "What do you have in there?"

"A bunch of food. Cupcakes. Chicken," Habib said. "My mother doesn't want me to starve."

Lucky, Mitchell thought.

Habib leaned over. "My mother put in Bugs Be Gone, too. Nothing will go near it."

"Does it work for snakes and bears?" Mitchell asked.

"It works for everything," Habib said. "Don't worry. I'll share."

Mitchell nodded. Habib was a great friend.

Mitchell climbed onto the bus. Too bad his mother didn't know Habib's mother. Mitchell's bag was filled with clothes.

All his mother was worried about was clean underwear and dry feet.

The bus started up.

It wouldn't be a long trip. The Zigzag Nature Center wasn't far.

"We can't walk, though," Ellie had said. "We have too much to carry. Tents, and food, and nets."

Nets?

Were they going to capture something? Mitchell hoped the nets were ant-sized.

He looked out the window. Maybe it would rain again.

He poked Habib. "Do you think we'll go home if it rains?"

Mrs. Farelli turned around. "Don't be silly, Mitchell. Zigzag kids are tough."

Mitchell put on his Gary Bopper face. "Rain is good," he said. "Rain is terrific."

How many hours were there in a day? Maybe sixty?

Gary Bopper would have his hands on his hips. He'd shout something. What? Maybe "Bears beware!"

The bus screeched to a stop.

"Everyone off," called the bus driver.

Mitchell scrubbed at the dusty window. They weren't at the Nature Center. He could still see the school.

"The bus broke down," Habib said.

"We're almost there," Mr. Oakley said. "We'll have to walk."

"What about all this stuff?" Ellie asked.

"Don't worry," said Mrs. Farelli. "The Afternoon Center boys and girls are strong as bulls."

Lucky Mrs. Farelli. She looked like a bull. Big and tough. No animal would mess with her.

They climbed down from the bus. The bus driver threw out bags and boxes.

A minute later, Mitchell had one end of the boys' tent pole on his shoulder. Habib had the other end.

The tent pole was a hundred miles long. It must have weighed as much as Mrs. Farelli.

Besides, Habib was a little taller than Mitchell.

The tent pole slid all over the place.

Sumiko and Destiny were carrying the girls' tent pole. Lucky. Both girls were the same size.

Charlie had four bags on his back. He was bent over like an old man.

Angel carried two bags. One of them was Mitchell's. He could see the red tape.

"Let's go," Mr. Oakley said.

They marched along.

Mitchell could see Angel and Yolanda in front. Angel looked back. She was probably checking up on him already.

She tripped over Yolanda's feet.

The bags went flying.

The one with the red tape opened.

Mitchell could see his underwear hanging out. Mom had bought it for this trip.

He raced forward. Never mind the tent pole.

"Oof!" yelled Habib.

Mitchell darted around Destiny. He threw himself on the bag.

Behind him, Habib yelled, "Watch out!"

Something hit Mitchell in the back of his head.

"Oh, no!" Gina said. "They just broke the boys' tent pole."

CHAPTER 4

STILL SATURDAY MORNING

At last they reached the Nature Center. It was a wild kind of place. Fields. A pond. Trees. Mitchell crossed his fingers. He hoped there wouldn't be killer animals.

"Bears beware," he whispered in a Gary Bopper voice.

He looked up. The sun had come out. It was a hot sun. He was thirsty already.

He had a bottle of juice in his pocket. He took a slug. He shared the rest with Habib.

"Drop everything right here," Mr. Oakley said, "in front of the Critter Cabin."

"Great name for small creatures," Ellie said.

"The front door is open," Mr. Oakley said. "Make sure to visit the critters today."

"Dee-lightful," Gina said. "I'm crazy about ants."

Habib wiped his mouth. "I'm not so crazy about ants. All they do is run around on the ground."

Wasps were worse, Mitchell thought. He'd been stung once.

Angel had called him a baby for crying.

But that was two years ago.

Wait a minute. The Critter Cabin was huge. How big were those creatures, anyway?

Screened windows were all over the front. A giant critter with stingers might break out any minute.

One thing Mitchell knew. He wasn't going near that place.

"We might see a tarantula," Angel said. Her voice was strange. Maybe she was getting a cold.

Yolanda nodded. "What about black widow spiders? A bite from one of those babies and it's goodbye!"

Mitchell tried not to think about elephant-sized wasps. He tried not to think about killer black widows.

He looked at the tent pole. It was in pieces. Where would they sleep?

"A perfect Saturday for a campout," Mrs. Farelli said.

"Too bad there's no tent for the boys," Ellie said.

"A small problem," Mr. Oakley said.

A truck rolled into the Nature Center. One fender was dented. Mitchell thought the whole thing might fall apart any minute.

A man got out. He had a gray ponytail. He looked as old as his truck.

Next, a skinny kid slid out. He had a ponytail, too. A red one. He had something all around his mouth.

Oatmeal?

Yuck.

"That kid's a walk-ing cereal box," Habib said.

Mitchell and Habib began to laugh.

Mrs. Farelli snapped her fingers. "We don't need a pair of sillies here."

Mitchell edged behind Habib. He bit his lip hard.

He watched the man with the gray ponytail. The man gave Mrs. Farelli a hug. "I'm late," he said. "I'm sorry."

Mrs. Farelli smiled at him. "This is the head of the Steven Z. Zigzag Nature Center," she told everyone. "His name is"—she took a breath—"Mr. Adam Farelli."

She swiped at the oatmeal on the skinny kid's face. "This is Owen, my grandson. He's vis-iting from New Jersey. A very unusual boy."

"More like weird," Habib whispered.

Wow, Mitchell thought. *Mrs. Farelli has a husband and a grandson with matching pony-tails.*

Mitchell had always thought Mrs. Farelli lived alone. Her house would look like a class-room. Chairs would be lined up in the living room.

Mr. Adam Farelli rubbed his hands together. "Are you ready for the Great Nature Hunt?" he asked.

A nature hunt?

Mitchell guessed he was ready. Habib had great food. Habib had Bugs Be Gone.

They'd stick together like glue.

"Pick a partner," Mr. Farelli said. "My part-ner is the beautiful Mrs. Farelli."

Beautiful! Mitchell could hear Habib taking deep breaths. He was trying not to laugh again.

Everyone was picking a partner.

Mitchell didn't have to think about that. Habib was right next to him.

They were always partners.

But Mrs. Farelli pushed the ponytail kid toward him. "Owen will be a great partner for you, Mitchell," she said.

Owen opened his mouth. His teeth were covered with oatmeal globs.

Mitchell swallowed.

"Great," Owen said.

CHAPTER 5

SATURDAY AFTERNOON

Mitchell and Habib looked at each other. "Maybe we could be three partners," Mitchell said.

Mrs. Farelli held up two fingers. "Two by two," she said. "Like Noah's Ark."

"Right," said Mr. Adam Farelli. His ponytail bobbed up and down. He handed a pile of papers to Mitchell. "Would you pass these out, buddy?"

Mitchell began to give out the papers. He looked down at pictures of birds and plants.

A fat animal stared out at him.

Mitchell looked closer.

The animal's teeth were the size of a basketball.

Angel stood next to him. "Don't be a baby, now," she said.

Bears beware, Mitchell said in his head.

Behind Angel, Gina was humming an opera song.

Charlie put on giant sunglasses. "I made them myself," he said.

Mitchell leaned over. "Why don't you be Owen's partner?"

"Are you crazy?" Charlie said.

Mrs. Farelli frowned.

"I guess I'll be partners with Owen," Mitchell said.

"Good going," said Mr. Adam Farelli. "Look for everything you see on your paper. Check off each one when you find it."

"There will be prizes for sharp eyes," Mrs. Farelli said.

Owen was nodding. "I know what the prizes are."

"Never mind, Owen," she said.

Mr. Farelli leaned against his truck.

Mitchell waited for the fender to drop off.

Mr. Farelli held up his hand. "Look for something unusual."

Mitchell didn't want to be surprised. He wanted to be home watching television.

Mrs. Farelli nodded. "Keep your eyes peeled. Check the pictures. Keep away from poison ivy."

Mitchell would keep away from animals with teeth, too.

"Ready, set—" Mr. Farelli began.

Owen didn't wait for *go*.

He grabbed Mitchell's arm and took off.

"Don't forget," Mr. Farelli called. "Stay on the paths."

Mitchell stumbled along with Owen. He'd probably have black-and-blue marks later.

"We have to hurry!" Owen yelled. "We have to win."

They zigzagged down the paths.

Owen hopped over a rock.

Mitchell hopped too late. "Yeow!" he yelled.

His toe was probably broken in half.

At last Owen let go of his arm.

Mitchell took a couple of deep breaths. He bent down to rub his toe inside his sneaker.

"I know we'll win this," Owen said. "My grandmother said she'd give me a great partner."

Mitchell had a warm feeling in his chest.

Mrs. Farelli thought he was great!

Then he thought of Habib and Charlie. They'd have Bugs Be Gone all over them. They'd be eating chicken and cupcakes.

Mitchell looked around.

Were he and Owen lost?

Already?

He could just about see a corner of the Critter Cabin.

Owen leaned closer.

He still had oatmeal on his chin. There was a blob on his ear.

How did he eat, anyway?

"Guess what the prizes are," Owen said.

Mitchell thought. Something wonderful?

A couple of days off from school?

Owen grinned. "Oatmeal bars with raisins for dessert."

Gross, Mitchell thought.

"I helped my grandmother make them. Stuck my fingers in the dough a thousand times," Owen said. "I ate a bunch of raisins. The cookies are all wrapped up now so ants and things can't get to them."

Mitchell took a step away from him. It was too horrible to think about.

CHAPTER 6

STILL SATURDAY AFTERNOON

Mitchell walked along. He looked back.

What had happened to Owen?

He heard a clicking noise ahead. It was Trevor on his stilts. He was talking to his friend Clifton.

A moment later, the path disappeared.

Mitchell seemed to be going up a hill. There was a sign: DEER WALK.

He didn't see deer.

He saw a mess of weeds. He heard a mosquito.

His feet were sinking into mud.

Maybe that was one of Mr. Farelli's surprises.

He heard Angel crashing around. "Mitchell!" she screamed.

She'd be calling him a baby any minute.

He kept going down the other side.

He looked at his paper. The first picture was a sticker bush with berries.

Watch out, the paper said. *Stickers are sharp!*

Mitchell raised each foot high as he walked.

He kept his eyes peeled for stickers.

He kept his eyes peeled for other surprises. Snakes. Poison ivy. Coyotes.

He heard Gina humming an opera song.

And wasn't that Charlie talking to Habib?

"Wait up, guys!" Mitchell

yelled. He yelled quietly. He didn't want Angel to hear him.

He dashed through a bunch of weeds.

Yeow!

They weren't weeds. They were stickers.

He bent down to scratch his leg.

Never mind. He crossed the sticker bush off his list.

He couldn't hear Habib and Charlie anymore.

Everything was quiet.

No, not exactly quiet.

Birds chirped. A red one flew around.

Mitchell hoped it wasn't a bat.

He found a picture of the bird: a cardinal.

He checked it off.

He was getting as

smart as Gary Bopper. And brave, too. Out in the wilderness alone.

He began to whistle. Almost whistle. It was more like a windstorm.

Too bad. Everyone else in the world could whistle. Even Angel.

He heard something.

It wasn't a bird. Not unless the bird was a hundred pounds.

Mitchell stopped on one foot.

The sound stopped, too.

Was an animal stalking him?

Last night he'd watched a movie on TV. It was the scariest thing he'd ever seen.

Angel hadn't thought it was scary. She'd sat on the couch. She'd put polish all over her nails.

In the movie, the good guy had tried to hide. But he couldn't find a place.

Mitchell looked around. There was no place to hide here, either.

Run, then.

The guy on TV had tried to run, too.

He'd tripped and fallen off a cliff. He'd almost broken his arm off.

Something zoomed past Mitchell.

A bear? *Don't be scared,* Mitchell told himself. "Bears beware," he whispered.

He began to run.

He dashed around bushes.

He waded through plants.

It was a good thing there weren't any cliffs.

There was the animal! Right in front of him.

It was small, and it was round and fat.

The animal saw him, too. It stared with terrible little eyes. Then it dashed away on skinny legs.

Mitchell dashed away, too.

Right into a tree.

Oof. He felt as if his head were dented in.

He was like Mr. Farelli's old truck. A broken head. A broken toe.

Gary Bopper, he told himself about ten times. *Bears beware!*

He looked up at the tree. It was an oak tree. He knew that without looking at the picture on the paper.

He'd check it off if he didn't get eaten alive.

Behind the bushes, something was breathing hard.

He poked his head around the tree.

Owen Farelli!

Owen looked as if he'd been running a race. His face was almost as red as his ponytail.

"I've been looking all over for you," Owen said. "We're partners, remember?"

"Right," Mitchell said.

"Did you hear those strange sounds?" Owen asked.

Now what?

Mitchell shook his head.

"It must have been a huge animal," Owen said. "I'm glad I'm not afraid of anything."

Mitchell looked at Owen. Owen was skinny, but maybe he was tough. Gary Bopper tough.

Owen pulled out his paper. "I've checked off a bunch of things. A woodpecker. A squirrel's nest. Even a turtle down at the pond."

Better than just a red bird and an oak tree, Mitchell thought.

"We still need this guy." Owen pointed to a picture. It was a fat little animal with skinny legs. "A groundhog."

Mitchell took a breath. "I saw that!" He checked it off.

They were probably going to win the prize.

Oatmeal bars made by Owen. And half-eaten.

Never mind that. Mitchell was going to stick to Owen like glue until they got back to Mr. and Mrs. Farelli.

CHAPTER 7

ALMOST DARK

At last, everything was checked off.

It was a good thing. The sun was going down.

Mitchell headed for the field. Owen was right behind him.

Owen kept talking about raisins and oat-meal dough.

"I can't wait to win," he said.

Mitchell didn't want to think about oatmeal

bars. But there was something worse to think about.

Sleeping outside on the ground.

They stopped at the edge of the field.

The girls' tent was set up at one end. In front of the tent were picnic tables.

Mr. Oakley was building a fire. It was a great crackling thing.

Mr. Oakley must have watched the same movie Mitchell had watched. The good guy had built a fire. The animals had stayed away. You could see their huge eyes in the jungle.

Mitchell looked for Habib.

He wasn't at the fire. He wasn't at a picnic table.

Food was coming. The lunch lady carried trays back and forth.

Mrs. Farelli helped, too. She wore an apron that said ZIGZAG KIDS LIKE TO EAT!

She smiled when she saw Owen.

Mitchell was starving. He slid onto a bench. He made sure it was near the fire.

Away from animals.

He tried to take up a lot of room. He had to save space for Habib.

Where was Habib? And where was Charlie?

Owen slid in next to him.

Mr. Adam Farelli asked, "Any surprises?"

"I heard a bird sing," Destiny said. "It sounded like a cuckoo clock."

Angel opened her mouth. Then she shut it again.

"I think I saw a coyote," Gina said.

"It was probably a rabbit," Mr. Adam Farelli said.

Mitchell looked toward the end of the table. Trevor was sitting there. He had a big bandage on his forehead.

"I fell off the stilts," he said.

"Too bad," Mrs. Farelli said. "But it's good to try unusual things."

Next to Mitchell, Owen reached into his pocket. He pulled out a rolled-up paper.

The paper was filthy.

Inside was a pile of raisins.

They were probably filthy, too.

"I saved them from the oatmeal dough," Owen said. He began to laugh.

Horrible, Mitchell thought. But then he had another thought. "That's funny," he told Owen.

Owen held out the paper.

"I'd have to be starving to death to take one," Mitchell said.

And then they both were laughing.

Mitchell looked up at the Critter Cabin. Were those giant feelers in the window? Stingers?

The lunch lady came along with her tray. "Chicken tenders," she said.

Mitchell's mouth watered.

She dumped a pile on his plate.

They were green.

They tasted like grass.

"My surprise sauce," she said. "Unusual, right?"

Habib would say *weird.*

Mitchell scarfed it down. Gina would say *dee-lightful.*

He stood up. He still didn't see Habib and Charlie.

Suppose they were out in the woods?

Suppose they were lost?

It was really dark now. All except for Mr. Oakley's great fire. And lights tacked up in the trees.

"Gather around," Mr. Oakley called. "We'll tell stories."

Mr. Adam Farelli clapped his hands. "Don't forget the prizes," he said. "Oatmeal bars for everyone."

"I love oatmeal bars," Yolanda said.

"You can have mine," Mitchell said.

"Your brother is generous," Yolanda told Angel.

"Sometimes," Angel said.

Mitchell started toward the fire.

But then he stopped.

What was moving at the window in the Critter Cabin?

Not feelers.

Not a tarantula.

Probably nothing.

But still . . .

CHAPTER 8

SATURDAY NIGHT

Owen tapped Mitchell on the arm. "Something's up there in the Critter Cabin. I saw it move."

Mitchell looked toward the fire. "Maybe we should tell—"

But Mr. Oakley had begun a story about a woodsman. And Mr. Farelli was giving out cookies.

Mitchell took a step toward Mrs. Farelli.

She put her finger on her lips. She pointed to Mr. Oakley. "Shhh," she said.

Owen had wiggled his way in front of the fire.

Was Habib up there in the Critter Cabin? Was Charlie?

Locked in?

He looked around for Ellie.

He didn't see her.

What would Gary Bopper do?

Mitchell didn't have to think about that.

He knew what Gary would do.

He'd march straight up to the Critter Cabin. He'd save Habib and Charlie from—

Tarantulas?

Black widows?

Mitchell didn't march straight up to the Critter Cabin.

It took him forever to get there. He had to find his flashlight. Then it was one foot in front of the other. He looked into the dark woods. *Bears beware!*

Maybe the door was locked.

He crossed his fingers. He hoped so.

He'd go back to the fire. He'd wait until Mr. Oakley finished his story.

The door wasn't locked.

It was wide open.

Mitchell took a Gary Bopper breath.

He stepped inside.

There were plenty of lights, but no creatures.

Not yet, he told himself.

At the end of a long hallway were stairs.

"Hey, Habib," he called.

His voice sounded odd. Just like Angel's had before. Maybe he was getting a cold, too.

He knew he wasn't getting a cold. *Gary Bopper,* he told himself.

"Hey, Charlie," he called.

No one answered.

They were probably upstairs.

Mitchell went up. He could hear his sneakers flapping on the wood.

There was a big room with glass cages. He saw one with an anthill. "Dee-lightful," he whispered.

He saw another with a lizard. A very large lizard.

He stopped to look at it.

The lizard blinked lazily.

He blinked back at it.

Where were Habib and Charlie?

He saw a case with lots of dead leaves. A few beetles were rushing around.

Mitchell went to the window. He could feel a breeze. A plant with long leaves waved back and forth on the sill.

That was what he'd seen outside.

He could see the fire now. He could almost hear Mr. Oakley telling his story.

Destiny was playing with her hair beads.

Yolanda was covering her ears. It must be a scary story.

Something was moving through the trees.

Downstairs, the door slammed.

"Habib?" he called.

No one could hear him. Not even the lizard, which was two inches away.

CHAPTER 9

STILL SATURDAY NIGHT

"Is that you, Mitchell?"

The voice was tiny.

He took a breath. Was that Angel?

Yes. It was only Angel.

Whew!

She came up the stairs, one step at a time.

She poked her head in the doorway. "Did you see any black widow spiders?"

He shook his head. "Not even one."

"What are you doing in this scary place?"

Mitchell blinked like the lizard. "I thought you weren't afraid of anything."

"I'm not afraid of regular things," she said. "Like scary movies . . ." She tiptoed to the window. "I'm afraid of lobsters."

"Lobsters are scary," Mitchell said.

"And snapping turtles."

"I guess so." Mitchell thought scary movies were worse.

"I was scared all day," Angel said. "I looked for you. I hoped you were all right."

Sometimes Angel surprised him. "Thanks," he said.

He was sorry he hadn't stuck to her like glue.

"I can't find Habib or Charlie," he said.

"I know where they are," she said. "I can't tell you."

"Why not?"

She raised one shoulder. "Look at the fireflies out there."

"Did Habib go home?" he asked. Maybe Habib was afraid, too.

Angel put her hand over her mouth. "I'm not supposed to tell."

"Not fair," he said.

She didn't answer.

Mitchell looked at the fireflies. He'd never seen this many.

Trevor was jumping around. He was trying to catch them in a jar.

The woods didn't seem so scary now. Not so big!

Mitchell could see the road.

A car was coming. The headlights were shining.

He and Angel went downstairs and out the door.

Owen walked over to them. "Hey, guys, did you see any black widows?"

"Not even one," Angel said.

Owen took a step closer. "I'm not afraid of them anyway."

He looked toward the woods. "We have to watch out for that animal. The one with that weird sound. It's almost like whistling."

Angel took a step back. "Whistling?"

"It must be huge," Owen said.

Mitchell tried to think. What could it be? Did bears whistle? No.

"That's why I didn't come with you," Owen said. "I wanted to stick close to the fire."

The car pulled up to the field.

Was that his mother's car?

Was that his dog, Maggie?

Habib and Charlie were getting out of the backseat.

"Hide your eyes," Angel said. "You're not supposed to look."

Mitchell closed his eyes.

He could hear a second car coming.

No, it wasn't a car. It sounded like a truck. It was bumping all over the place.

He opened one eye. It was Mr. Adam Farelli's truck. A long pole stuck out of the back.

A tent pole.

Mr. Oakley was helping him with it.

The boys wouldn't have to sleep on the bare ground with snakes or lizards.

Mitchell didn't even mind lizards anymore.

He opened his other eye.

Habib and Charlie were carrying a box. Maggie was jumping around them.

"I know they're going to drop it," Angel said.

"What is it?" he asked.

"Close your eyes," she said again. "I don't want you to see the cake smashed on the ground."

"What cake?" he asked.

She didn't answer. But she didn't have to.

Mitchell had figured it out.

It was his birthday cake! One day early.

Habib was trying to keep it steady.

Then Mitchell did close his eyes.

He knew what was going to happen.

Down at the fire, he could hear Mrs. Farelli say, "Oh, no!"

CHAPTER 10

SUNDAY MORNING

What was that clanging noise in his ear?

Maybe it was the whistling animal.

Mitchell tried to move. His arms were caught. So were his legs.

Was he in a giant web?

He opened his eyes.

Huge eyes looked down at him.

Animal eyes.

Maggie's eyes. Whew!

Mitchell remembered everything at once.

Maggie had stuck to him like glue last night. Mrs. Farelli had said that she could stay.

The noise he heard wasn't an animal. It was Mr. Farelli. He was clanging a bell. "Up and at 'em," he called. "Breakfast at the Zigzag Pond."

Best of all, it was Mitchell's birthday. There'd be a special dinner at home later. Fried chicken fingers and ice cream. A bunch of presents.

But now they marched to the pond. They marched slowly. Trevor was back on his stilts.

Today Owen had blue stuff around his mouth.

"It's icing from your birthday cake," Habib told Mitchell.

Mitchell nodded. It had been the best cake: chocolate with blue and white icing.

Too bad it had fallen upside down. They'd flipped it back over. The top had said *HAP B MIT.*

Mitchell grinned. *Happy birthday, Mitchell.*

This morning the pond sparkled. Two ducks swam on the water.

Mrs. Farelli flapped out blankets so they could sit.

The lunch lady gave them bananas, yogurt, and a bread thing. It had little green chunks. It was the same snack as the other day.

"Celery," Owen said.

"Stick to me like glue, Mitchell," Angel whispered.

"Don't worry," he said.

Angel didn't think he was a baby anymore. Maybe it was because he was one year older today.

He watched a huge turtle on a log.

A snapping turtle?

It didn't scare him. Besides, it was at the other end of the pond.

Mitchell sat back. He felt the sun on his face.

It was a great day. A terrific day.

He felt like Gary Bopper.

He tried a little whistle.

It sounded like the wind.

He had to keep trying.

Next to him, Owen began to scream. "There it is! That weird animal."

"Baby," Angel said. "It's just Mitchell. He's learning how to whistle."

"Not an animal after all," Owen said. "Whew!"

"Whew," Mitchell said, too. He tried another whistle.

There was a huge splash.

"Oh, no!" Angel yelled. "Here comes a snapper."

Mitchell leaned forward. The turtle hadn't moved.

It was Trevor.

He had fallen into the pond.

Mitchell watched Mr. Oakley pull him out.

Mitchell sat back. He had just realized something. He liked campouts.

Lots of surprises.

And no bears.

PATRICIA REILLY GIFF is the author of many beloved books for children, including the Kids of the Polk Street School books, the Friends and Amigos books, and the Polka Dot Private Eye books. Several of her novels for older readers have been chosen as ALA-ALSC Notable Children's Books and ALA-YALSA Best Books for Young Adults. They include *The Gift of the Pirate Queen; All the Way Home; Water Street; Nory Ryan's Song,* a Society of Children's Book Writers and Illustrators Golden Kite Honor Book for Fiction; and the Newbery Honor Books *Lily's Crossing* and *Pictures of Hollis Woods. Lily's Crossing* was also chosen as a *Boston Globe–Horn Book* Honor Book. Her most recent books for older readers include *R My Name Is Rachel, Storyteller, Wild Girl,* and *Eleven.* Other books in the Zigzag Kids series include *Number One Kid, Big Whopper, Flying Feet,* and *Star Time.* Patricia Reilly Giff lives in Connecticut.

Patricia Reilly Giff is available for select readings and lectures. To inquire about a possible appearance, please contact the Random House Speakers Bureau at rhspeakers@randomhouse.com.

ALASDAIR BRIGHT is a freelance illustrator who has worked on numerous books and advertising projects. He loves drawing and is never without his sketchbook. He lives in Bedford, England.